# KILLERS

# PREHISTORIC ANIMALS

## PHILIP STEELE

**Julian Messner**

First published by Heinemann Children's Reference,
a division of Heinemann Educational Books Ltd
Original Copyright © 1991 Heinemann Educational Books Ltd

Published by Julian Messner, a division of
Silver Burdett Press, Inc., Simon & Schuster, Inc.
Prentice Hall Bldg., Englewood Cliffs, NJ 07632

JULIAN MESSNER and colophon are trademarks of
Simon & Schuster, Inc.
U.S. project editor: Nancy Furstinger

Printed in Hong Kong

Lib. ed. 10 9 8 7 6 5 4 3 2 1
Paper ed. 10 9 8 7 6 5 4 3 2 1

**Library of Congress Cataloging-in-Publication Data**
Steele, Philip.
  Killers – prehistoric animals/Philip Steele.
    p.  cm.
  Summary: Discusses prehistoric animals that were savage or
  dangerous, from early fishes and reptiles through the dinosaurs to
  the time of the big mammals and the two-legged hunters.
  1. Animals, Fossil – Juvenile literature. 2. Predatory animals –
  Juvenile literature. [1. Prehistoric animals.] I. Title.
  QE765.S74   1991
  566 – dc20                                        90-34766
                                                       CIP
                                                        AC

  ISBN 0-671-72241-7 ISBN 0-671-72242-5 (pbk.)

**Photographic Acknowledgments**
The author and publishers wish to acknowledge, with thanks, the following photographic sources:
*a* above *b* below *l* left *r* right
Cover photograph courtesy of Ardea (A Hayward)
Ardea pp7*a* (P Morris), 7*b* (A Hayward), 17*a* & *b*, 21, 25 (A Hayward), 22 (Francois Gohier); Science Photograph Library p4 (Julian
Baum); Topham Picture Library p31; Werner Forman Archive p30.
The publishers have made every effort to trace the copyright holders, but if they have inadvertently overlooked any, they will be pleased
to make the necessary arrangement at the first opportunity.

# CONTENTS

# TOOTH AND CLAW

S OME of the first animals on Earth were fierce. These prehistoric ancestors of today's warm- and cold-blooded animals killed to defend themselves, to protect their young, or to get food.

We shall go back millions of years, to the time before humans developed on our planet. We shall look at some of the huge creatures that lived in jungles, swamps, and seas.

## THE TIME SCALE OF TERROR

I F an animal is to survive, it must be able to get food and to stay warm. Many prehistoric animals survived by eating other animals. Others ate plants and survived by running, swimming, flying, or hiding.

As conditions changed, new kinds of animals developed. This process of change is called evolution. It takes a very long time for creatures to change, or evolve. Simple life forms first appeared in the seas more than 45 billion years ago. The first true animals appeared about 570 million years ago.

We know how life forms evolved because animals have left traces of their existence in layers of rock. Rocks of different time periods have been given the names shown in the chart. The periods have been grouped together into geological time units called eras.

| Era | Million of years ago | Period | |
|-----|---------------------|--------|---|
| Cenozoic | 2 | Pleistocene | |
| | 5 | Pliocene | |
| | 25 | Miocene | Age of mammals |
| | 37 | Oligocene | |
| | 55 | Eocene | |
| | 65 | Palaeocene | |
| Mesozoic | 136 | Cretaceous | |
| | 190 | Jurassic | Age of reptiles |
| | 225 | Triassic | |
| Palaeozoic | 280 | Permian | |
| | 345 | Carboniferous | Age of amphibians |
| | 395 | Devonian | Age of fish |
| | 430 | Silurian | |
| | 500 | Ordovician | Age of sea creatures |
| | 570 | Cambrian | |

# TRACKING THE ANCIENT KILLERS

T RACES of animals that lived millions of years ago can still be found. Some remains or shapes of animals were preserved in rock. They are called fossils. Some fossils are just footprints made in mud that later hardened. Other fossils are the shapes made by the bodies of dead animals as they sank into mud. The mud hardened and new layers of rock built up over the fossils. Over the ages, the Earth moved and the fossils shifted. Fossils that had been beneath the ocean floor or underground came to the surface.

The bodies of some prehistoric animals have been preserved in swamps or frozen soil.

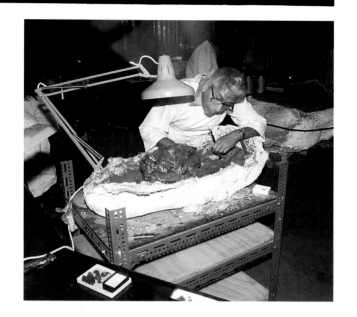

## Animal weapons

By studying fossilized teeth, skeletons, and horns, scientists can tell how prehistoric animals lived. They can tell what the animals ate, how they hunted, and how fast they ran. We shall look at the weapons evolved by killer animals.

(A) skull of *Tyrannosaurus*

(B) *Allosaurus* claw

(C) horns of *Triceratops*

(D) tail of *Stegosaurus*

# THE FIRST SHARKS

T HE most feared fish today are the sharks. Their prehistoric ancestors would have seemed even more frightening. Fossils show that they were very large.

## THE BIG CRUNCH

F ISH first evolved about 500 million years ago. Many early fish did not have jaws. They sucked up food from the bottom of seas and lakes. Later, a group of fish with real jaws developed. They were called placoderms. The biggest was *Dunkleostus*. It was 30 feet long and lived in the Devonian Period. It is also known as dinichthys, which means "terrible fish." The front of its body was armored. Its teeth were jagged, razor-sharp pieces of bone.

*Dunkleostus* (dinichthys)

# THE SHARKS MOVE IN

O VER many millions of years, all kinds of primitive fish developed. Some were ancestors of the modern sharks.

The biggest prehistoric fish of all was a shark related to the modern great white shark. It is called *Carcharodon megalodon*. It lived about 15 million years ago, in the Tertiary Period. Its jaws were almost 9 feet wide and could open 6 feet. The largest of its teeth, found near Bakersfield, California, is almost 6 inches long. The shark must have been more than 52 feet long!

*Carcharodon megalodon*

# FROM WATER TO LAND

ETWEEN 345 and 395 million years ago, some fish had developed lungs. They could take in oxygen directly from the air. Most fish took oxygen from the water. Later, animals that could live on land and in water developed. These were the first amphibians.

## The first land-dweller

*Ichthyostega* is the first creature we know of that walked on land on 4 legs. It lived about 350 million years ago, in lakes and pools. It was about 3 feet long and hunted fish. Its remains were found in Greenland.

*Ichthyostega*

*Diplovertebron*

## Hunters of the swamps

*Diplovertebron* lived in swamps about 300 million years ago. One species lived in Europe, and another in North America. Each was about 24 inches long.

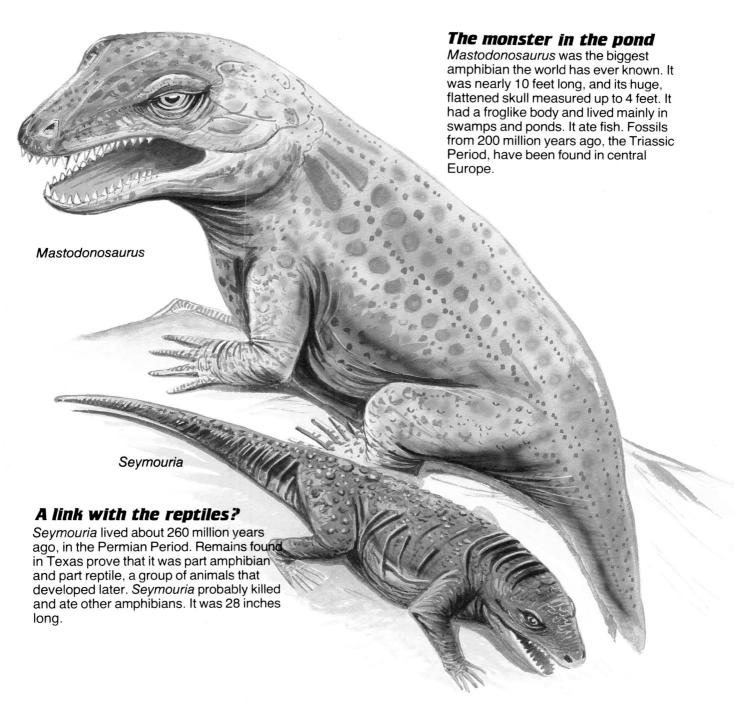

## The monster in the pond

*Mastodonosaurus* was the biggest amphibian the world has ever known. It was nearly 10 feet long, and its huge, flattened skull measured up to 4 feet. It had a froglike body and lived mainly in swamps and ponds. It ate fish. Fossils from 200 million years ago, the Triassic Period, have been found in central Europe.

*Mastodonosaurus*

*Seymouria*

## A link with the reptiles?

*Seymouria* lived about 260 million years ago, in the Permian Period. Remains found in Texas prove that it was part amphibian and part reptile, a group of animals that developed later. *Seymouria* probably killed and ate other amphibians. It was 28 inches long.

# REPTILES RULE THE WORLD

M ANY prehistoric amphibians were so good at living on land that they evolved into a totally new kind of animal. From about 280 to 65 million years ago, reptiles were the most important form of life on Earth. Some later evolved into birds and mammals. Others continued to evolve as reptiles. Many prehistoric reptiles were harmless. Others were dangerous.

## What is a reptile?

Reptiles are crawling animals, with short legs, like lizards, or with none at all, like snakes. They lay eggs and are cold-blooded. This means that they cannot control the heat of their bodies. About 5,175 kinds of reptiles live in the world today.

## The toothy smile

*Dimetrodon* had curving jaws packed with teeth designed for biting, gripping, and slashing. It was an aggressive, quick-moving reptile. It had a spiny sail running along its back. This evolved as a simple way to control body heat. Remains found in Texas and Oklahoma show that *Dimetrodon* was up to 10 feet long. It lived about 260 million years ago.

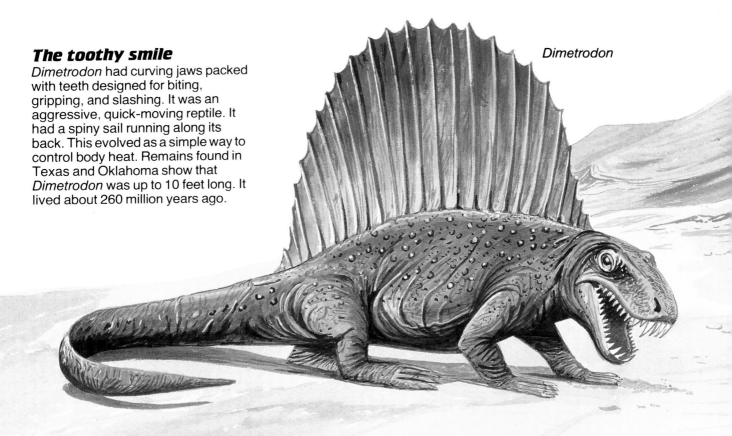

*Dimetrodon*

## Terror of the herds

*Lycaenops* lived in southern Africa during the Permian Period. It was an aggressive reptile about 3 feet long. Its name means "wolf-faced." It had sharp chopping teeth and long, stabbing canines. It ate plant-eating reptiles.

*Lycaenops*

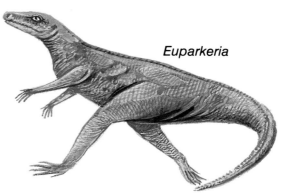

*Euparkeria*

## The savage beast

*Sauroctonus* lived about 250 million years ago, in eastern Europe. It was about 10 feet long. It had huge front teeth that could rip flesh from its prey.

*Sauroctonus*

13

# THE FIRST CROCODILES

**M**YSTRIOSAURUS lived in the warm seas of the Jurassic Period, more than 180 million years ago. It is an ancestor of today's crocodiles. Its 13-foot-long body was covered with armor plating. Its long snout was lined with sharp teeth. These were used to grip and tear apart the fish and other sea creatures it ate.

## SEA KILLER

**T**HE remains of another crocodile were found in the Jurassic rocks of western Europe. *Metriorhynchus* lived about 150 million years ago. Instead of webbed feet, it had paddles. It swam with its long, fishlike tail. This reptile caught fish with its three pairs of extra-large teeth. Its unarmored body was 8 feet long. Sea crocodiles with no armor plating soon died out.

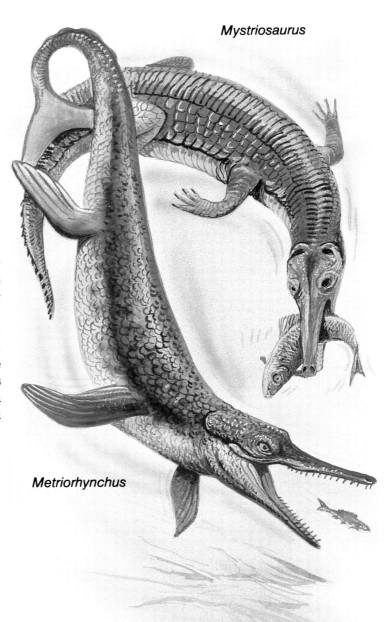

Mystriosaurus

Metriorhynchus

# KING OF THE CROCS

**T**HE biggest crocodile of all lived about 75 million years ago in Montana and Texas. *Deinosuchus* had a 6-foot skull and was more than 49 feet long.

Thin-snouted fish-eating crocodiles called gharials have been found in 7-million-year-old rocks in the United States and India. They were nearly as long as *Deinosuchus*.

# DEADLY DINOSAURS

D URING the Triassic Period, about 225 million years ago, new kinds of reptiles began to appear. We call them dinosaurs. They were reptiles, but most could walk and run more easily than their ancestors.

There were two main groups of dinosaurs. One group had hipbones like those of birds. They were plant-eaters. Most moved slowly. Many of them were huge and had armor plating, horns, and spikes. The other group of dinosaurs had hipbones like those of lizards. Some of these were plant-eating giants. *Brachiosaurus* was 75 feet long, and *Diplodocus* even longer. Others were meat-eaters. They included some of the scariest killers ever.

## THE EGG-STEALER

O RNITHOMIMUS was a lizard-hipped dinosaur of the Cretaceous Period. It belonged to a group of dinosaurs that had no teeth. Instead, it had beaky jaws. It ate the eggs and young of other dinosaurs. It looked like an ostrich, and ran quickly.

★ The word "dinosaur" was invented in 1841. It means "terrible lizard."

# THE TYRANT KING

*T*YRANNOSAURUS rex ("king tyrant-lizard") roamed the Earth more than 70 million years ago. It was a huge, very strong lizard-hipped dinosaur. It was 46 feet long and more than 18 feet tall. Its skull measured 4½ feet. Its jaws held saw-edged teeth up to 6 inches long. It ate large, plant-eating dinosaurs.

## The end of an era
About 65 million years ago, the age of the dinosaurs ended. We do not know why. Perhaps Earth was hit by a meteorite, and this caused the climate to change. Perhaps the plants they ate disappeared. Maybe too many dinosaur eggs were eaten by newer kinds of creatures known as mammals.

# THE OGRE

*A*LLOSAURUS could be just as savage as *Tyrannosaurus*. It grew 40 feet long and lived in Montana and Wyoming. The skull was about 28 inches long. It had about 72 teeth that slanted backward. Its jaw could open wide so it could gulp down very large pieces of flesh. It lived about 150 million years ago and hunted plant-eating dinosaurs.

# SEA MONSTERS

A LL land animals evolved from water creatures. Over the ages, some animals returned to a life in the sea. Some of these grew to look like fish, while others looked more like turtles. During the Jurassic and Cretaceous Periods sea reptiles called plesiosaurs appeared.

## THE LONG-NECKED SNAPPERS

T HE biggest of the plesiosaurs is known as *Elasmosaurus*. It was 43 feet long, and had a coiling, 23-foot-long neck made up of 76 bones. No other animal, including a giraffe, has had a neck this long. The reptile paddled through the water, hunting fish and squid. It even may have plucked flying lizards from the sky. It had a dangerous-looking snout and long, sharp front teeth. An 80-million-year-old fossil of one was found in Kansas.

*Elasmosaurus*

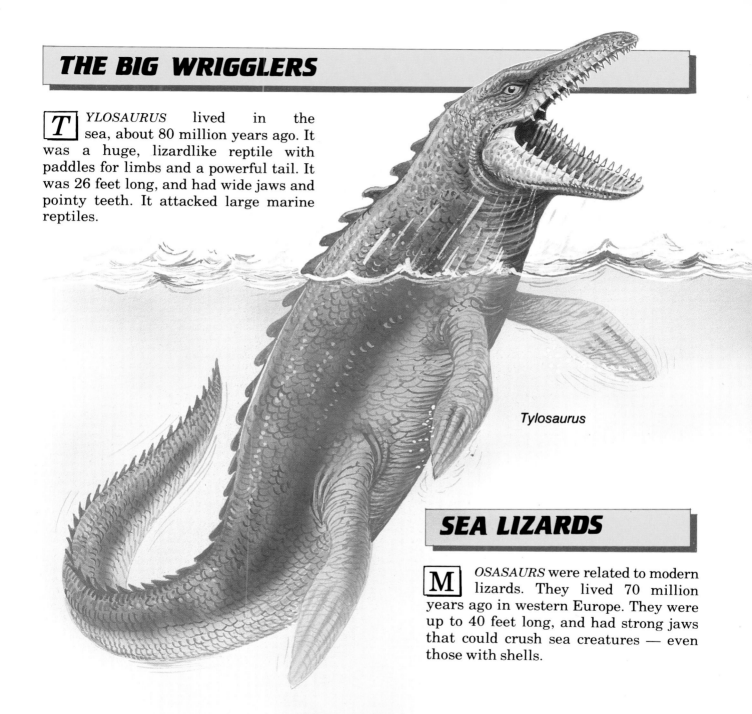

# THE BIG WRIGGLERS

*T*YLOSAURUS lived in the sea, about 80 million years ago. It was a huge, lizardlike reptile with paddles for limbs and a powerful tail. It was 26 feet long, and had wide jaws and pointy teeth. It attacked large marine reptiles.

*Tylosaurus*

# SEA LIZARDS

*M*OSASAURS were related to modern lizards. They lived 70 million years ago in western Europe. They were up to 40 feet long, and had strong jaws that could crush sea creatures — even those with shells.

19

# FLYING LIZARDS

D URING the late Triassic Period, about 200 million years ago, some reptiles developed wings for gliding. They are known as pterosaurs, which means "winged lizards."

*Dimorphodon* was a winged lizard. A skeleton of one was found on the English coast. It lived in the Jurassic Period, about 175 million years ago. It had a heavy skull that was more than 8½ inches long, and large teeth. It may have hunted fish. Its long tail helped it to balance and steer. The flapping, leathery wings measured 5 feet across. We do not know if *Dimorphodon* could really fly or if it could only glide. It may have lived on the ground.

About 150 million years ago a strange-looking pterosaur was swooping over lakes in search of fish. *Rhamphorhynchus* had a snout like a beak that was lined with jagged spikes. Its long tail, which gave it a total length of about 12 inches, was used for steering. A fossil of one was found in Jurassic rocks in southern Germany.

★ **The largest flying creature ever known was the pterosaur *Quetzalcoatlus*. Its wingspan must have been 39 to 50 feet. It lived in the Cretaceous Period, and may have scavenged for food like vultures do.**

*Dimorphodon*

*Rhamphorhynchus*

# "FEATHERED DINOSAURS"

R OUGHLY 150 million years ago, some flying reptiles evolved into the first birds. One of these, *Archaeopteryx,* still had much in common with reptiles. Instead of a beak, it had jaws with small teeth. It had claws at the front of its wings and a long tail. Otherwise, it was a true bird. It had feathers and sharp, curved claws on its legs. It could glide over short distances.

## GIGANTIC BIRDS

B IRDS began to fly and still do. Huge birds, such as vultures with wingspans of more than 23 feet, evolved. The biggest birds could not fly. They survived by running quickly from danger.

Some flightless birds were fierce meat-eaters. *Phororharcos* used it large hooked beak to kill reptiles and mammals. It was up to 10 feet tall and had a huge skull 2 feet long. It lived about 20 million years ago in Patagonia, in South America.

*Phororharcos*

# SUPERSNAKES

S NAKES are the most recent reptiles to appear on Earth. They first lived in the Cretaceous Period, and probably evolved from monitor lizards. There are very few fossils of snakes. Their small skulls were often crushed, and their skeletons were often broken and scattered. The ancestors of snakes may have been burrowers. Their long, thin, legless bodies would have moved easily through the soil.

Snakes had jaws that were held together loosely. They could open wide and swallow large prey whole. Fangs that slopped backward stopped the victim from escaping.

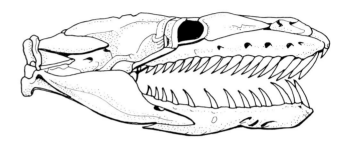

Python skull

## SQUEEZE OF DEATH

P YTHONS and boas belong to the oldest group of snakes. They are called constrictors. These snakes wrap their bodies around their prey and squeeze until it chokes to death.

Boa constrictor

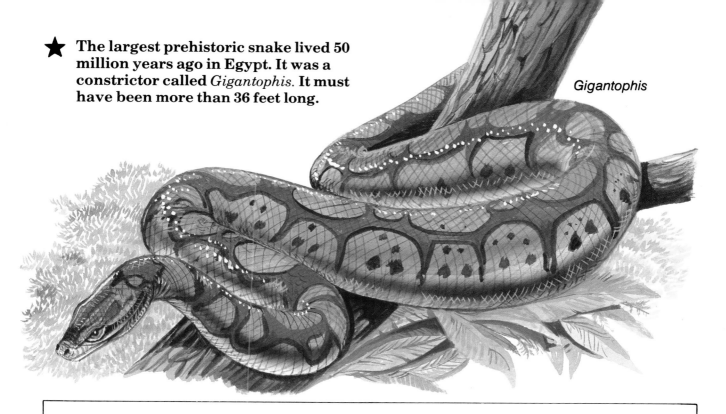

★ The largest prehistoric snake lived 50 million years ago in Egypt. It was a constrictor called *Gigantophis*. It must have been more than 36 feet long.

*Gigantophis*

## DEATH BY POISON

D URING the Tertiary Period, new kinds of snakes, called colubrids, evolved. Their jaws could swallow prey even more easily than those of the constrictors. About 300 of today's snakes belong to this group.

Many developed poison fangs. They also evolved better ways of injecting venom. Some adapted to live in the sea.

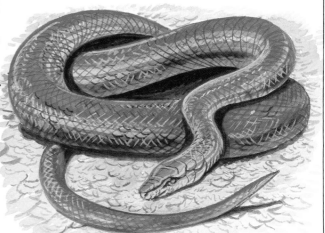

# THE AGE OF MAMMALS

A BOUT 220 million years ago, some reptiles were evolving into mammals. These were warm-blooded and covered with hair. They had one lower jawbone. Today, mammals are the most successful form of life on Earth. Most mammals give birth to live young. Babies feed on the mother's milk.

The first mammals were small animals, similar to shrews. Larger mammals evolved 160 million years later.

## HEAVYWEIGHTS

T HE biggest prehistoric mammals were herbivores, or animals that feed on plants. Some were so huge that few animals could have beaten them in a fight.

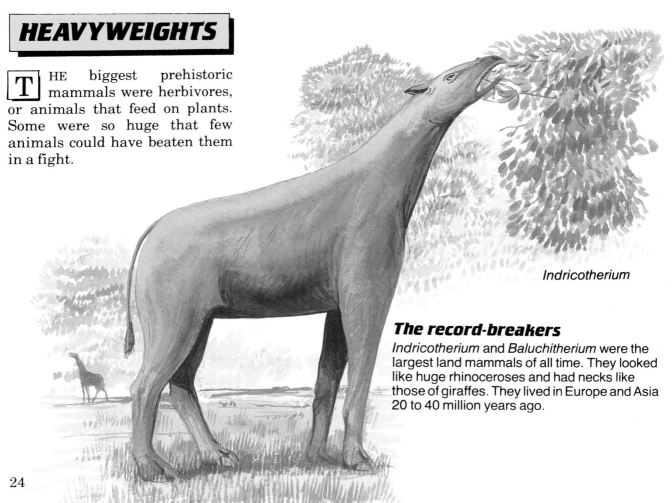

*Indricotherium*

### The record-breakers
*Indricotherium* and *Baluchitherium* were the largest land mammals of all time. They looked like huge rhinoceroses and had necks like those of giraffes. They lived in Europe and Asia 20 to 40 million years ago.

## A giant rhino

*Elasmotherium* was a rhinoceros. It was bigger than any living now. It lived on the grasslands of the southern Soviet Union 200,000 to 230,000 years ago. It had a 6½-foot horn on its head.

## The woolly mammoth

Many prehistoric mammals looked like today's elephants. The woolly mammoth stood about 15 feet tall and was 18 feet long. It lived in cold northern lands and had a warm, shaggy coat. Its huge curved tusks could be more than 16 feet long. It was stalked by stone-age hunters and there are cave paintings of it. Frozen remains were found in the ice of Siberia.

# SAVAGES

NDREWSARCHUS lived in Mongolia, in Asia, about 40 million years ago. It was 13 feet long and 6½ feet high at the shoulder. It had the biggest skull of any meat-eater. The skull was four times the size of a modern wolf's. Its long, snarling muzzle was lined with rounded teeth that cracked bones. It could rapidly tear apart a dead animal. Like today's bears, it probably ate plants and roots as well as meat.

## THE FIRST KILLER CATS

DINICTIS was an early type of wildcat that looked like a small leopard. It had large canine teeth. Its body was a little more than 3 feet long, and it was about 2 feet high. This fierce little hunter lived in North America about 30 million years ago.

# POUCHED KILLERS

ONE group of mammals evolved a special way of raising its young. Babies stayed in a pouch outside the mother's body until they could look after themselves. Some pouched animals, or marsupials, survive today. Koalas, kangaroos, and opossums are examples.

Thylacosmilus

Borhyaena

*Thylacosmilus* was a meat-eating marsupial that looked like a big cat. It was up to 10 feet in length and had long, pointed fangs. It lived in South America between 3 and 5 million years ago.

*Borhyaena* was another South American marsupial. It looked like a cross between a small puma and a bear. It was 3 feet long. It did not move fast, but its strong teeth could tear flesh rapidly and crack bones.

# SABER TEETH

S OME of the most famous prehistoric killers are known as saber-toothed tigers. The name is used for various catlike mammals that hunted herds between 3 million and 400,000 years ago. Remains of one type, *Homotherium*, were found in eastern Europe and southern Asia. Remains of another, *Smilodon* were found in South America.

These tigers had a terrible snarl. They could open their jaws to a right angle. Their curving canine teeth were about 6 inches long and were used to rip prey apart.

*Homotherium*

# LONE HUNTERS OF THE ICE AGES

B ONES and paintings of very large lions have been found in European caves. The lions hunted alone and preyed on wild horses. They seem to have had no manes, but they did have thick, furry coats to protect them from the bitter cold weather. Cave lions lived between about 350,000 and 10,000 years ago. During this time, called the Ice Ages, ice from the Arctic covered much of the Northern Hemisphere.

Cave lion

# GIANT BEARS

THE first bears evolved from doglike mammals. Unlike the dogs, the bears ate plants as well as meat.

The cave bear lived in Eurasia between 270,000 and 20,000 years ago. It fed mostly on berries and roots, but it probably fought when humans disturbed it in its den. They hunted bears for their fur, meat, and fat. Cave bears died out because of changes in the climate.

# THE TWO-LEGGED HUNTERS

A creature that can be among the most efficient killers had harmless origins. About 40 million years ago, the first monkeys evolved. They lived in trees. About 30 million years ago, more-intelligent mammals, called apes, evolved from this group. The ancestors of humans evolved from relatives of the apes. They moved from a life in the trees to a life on the plains. The remains of *Australopithecus*, a humanlike mammal that lived in Africa, helps us guess at their way of life.

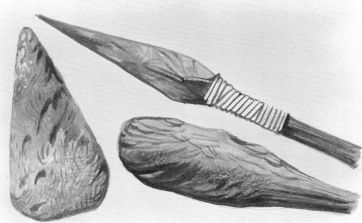

Stone-age weapons

## MAKERS OF WEAPONS

H OMO habilis ("handy man") appeared in East Africa about 2 million years ago. This early human used simple tools and weapons. *Homo erectus* ("upright man") made fire and hunted large animals in Africa, Asia, China, and Europe between 1.5 million and 200,000 years ago. Neanderthal people lived in Europe, Asia, and North Africa 100,000 years ago. They were even smarter. *Homo sapiens* ("wise man") were common from about 400,000 years ago onward.

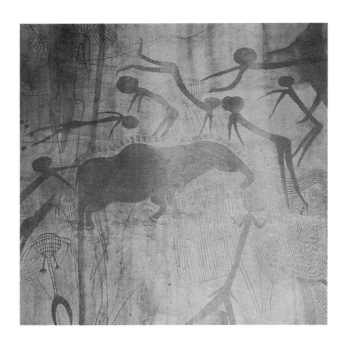

Cave painting of prehistoric hunters

# THE CHALLENGE OF SURVIVAL

H UMANS were successful because they evolved limbs that helped them to run, and fingers that could grip and make tools and weapons. They also evolved brains that could reason and explore. This raised them above the level of other animals. It also made them possibly dangerous killers. They did not have claws, horns, or poison fangs; but they could make weapons.

We humans have invented many wonderful things. However, some humans have also killed each other and destroyed many animals. Luckily we are intelligent enough to learn from our mistakes. We must have more respect for each other and for other creatures. *Homo sapiens* must live up to the "wisdom" in our name, or become extinct like the dinosaurs.

# INDEX